Stories
and Songs for
Bedtime

For Lily

OXFORD
UNIVERSITY PRESS

Great Clarendon Street, Oxford OX2 6DP

Oxford University Press is a department of the University of Oxford.
It furthers the University's objective of excellence in research, scholarship,
and education by publishing worldwide in

Oxford   New York

Auckland   Cape Town   Dar es Salaam   Hong Kong   Karachi
Kuala Lumpur   Madrid   Melbourne   Mexico City   Nairobi
New Delhi   Shanghai   Taipei   Toronto

With offices in

Argentina   Austria   Brazil   Chile   Czech Republic   France   Greece
Guatemala   Hungary   Italy   Japan   Poland   Portugal   Singapore
South Korea   Switzerland   Thailand   Turkey   Ukraine   Vietnam

Oxford is a registered trade mark of Oxford University Press
in the UK and in certain other countries

Story texts and illustrations © Ian Beck 2004

The moral rights of the author/artist have been asserted

Database right Oxford University Press (maker)

First published in 2004
First published in paperback in 2006

British Library Cataloguing in Publication Data available

ISBN-13: 978-0-19-278198-7 (Hardback)
ISBN-10: 0-19-278198-7 (Hardback)
ISBN-13: 978-0-19-278228-1 (Paperback)
ISBN-10: 0-19-278228-2 (Paperback)

1 3 5 7 9 10 8 6 4 2

Printed in China

Rudyard Kipling: Seal Lullaby (1894) reprinted by permission of A. P. Watt Ltd
on behalf of The National Trust for Places of Historical Interest or Natural Beauty.

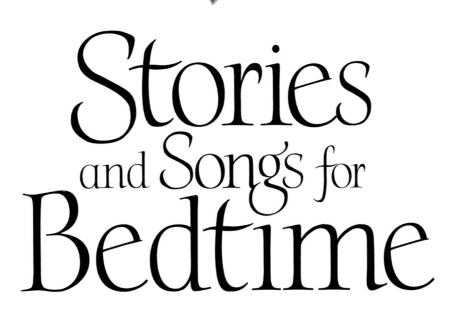

Stories
and Songs for
Bedtime

An illustrated treasury by

IAN BECK

OXFORD

CONTENTS

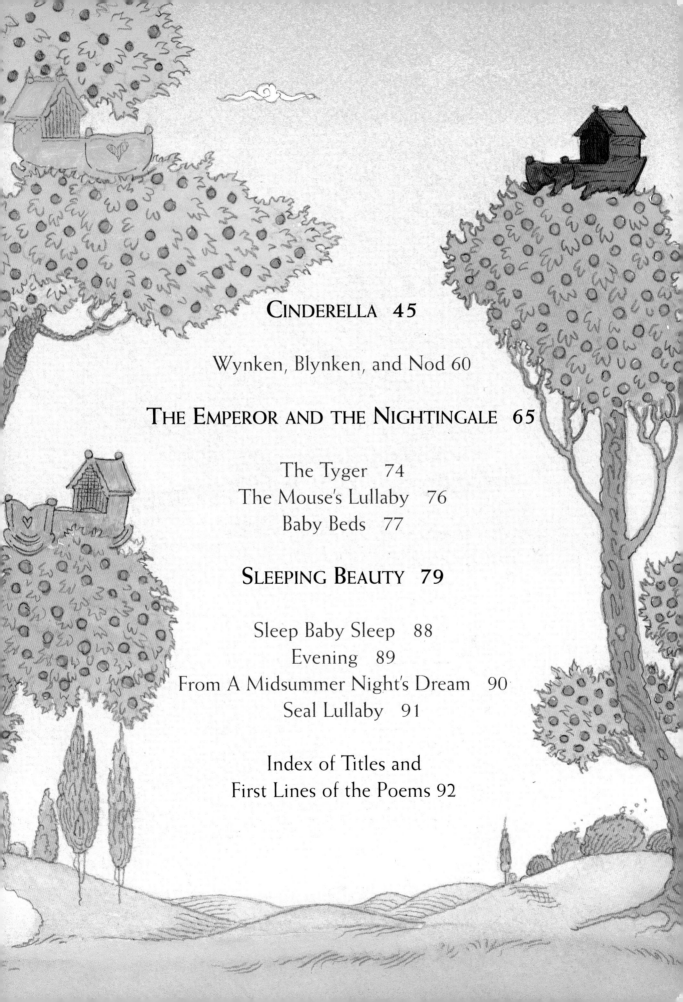

BEAUTY AND
THE BEAST

ONCE, IN A FARAWAY PLACE, there lived a merchant. He had been very rich, but storms had sunk all his ships, and he had lost his fortune.

The merchant had four daughters, who were used to beautiful things and fine clothes. Now they had to work and they complained bitterly. All except his younger daughter, Beauty, who was happy.

Autumn had just begun, when one day a messenger brought good news for the merchant. His fortune could be restored, but he would have to travel far away.

His daughters were delighted that their old life might return. They begged their father to bring them back fine presents from his travels.

All except Beauty. She asked only for her father's safe return. Her sisters were cross when they heard this. 'She's just trying to prove how nice she is,' they complained.

But their father smiled. 'There must be something I can bring you,' he said to Beauty.

'Well,' she said, 'what I should like most of all is a single white rose.'

'Then a white rose it shall be,' said the merchant.

All that autumn he traded in distant lands and cities. He bought all the gifts his daughters had asked for, but, try as he might, he could not find a white rose. For by now winter had set in. Snow swirled as the merchant made his way home through the dark forests. He could hear the terrifying howl of hungry wolves. The merchant shivered. He trudged on but the howling grew steadily louder, and nearer.

The merchant knew he must find shelter — and soon.

He stumbled on and, feeling something solid underfoot, looked up and saw a pair of tall, gilded gates. Snow had settled on them, but they glowed bright and golden in the lamplight. Beyond them, he could see a path lined with trees.

The trees were as green as summer, and oranges and lemons grew on their branches.

'How can this be?' whispered the merchant to himself. He opened the gates and walked up the marble path. Ahead, shrouded in mist, stood a huge castle. A warm light shone from its windows. 'Shelter at last,' he sighed, as he stabled his horse.

The castle door opened on to a long, grand hallway. 'Whoever lives here is rich indeed,' thought the merchant.

Then he called out, 'Is anybody there?'

He heard a low growl, like the purr of a lion, but he could see nothing. 'I seek only shelter,' he said, nervously.

He walked through a series of beautiful rooms, until he reached one where a sofa was pulled up close to the fire and a hearty supper was laid on a low table. The merchant had not eaten all day, so he quickly ate the delicious food and soon fell fast asleep.

The next morning he found a parlour where a table was set for breakfast. Above the fireplace hung a portrait of a handsome young man. 'My host, no doubt,' thought the merchant.

Later, he walked in the gardens where the air was warm, even though it was deep winter. The merchant shook his head, convinced the castle must be enchanted. There was no sign of his host.

He walked along a terrace to an ancient wall, which was covered by a sweet-smelling, climbing white rose.

The merchant thought at once of Beauty. 'My host couldn't begrudge me one of these,' he said to himself, and reached for the best bloom he could see.

Suddenly, he heard a huge roar. The merchant turned round in terror. There stood a beast; a beast with the body of a large and powerfully built man, dressed in fine clothes and draped in a black cloak.

'Why do you pick my roses?' growled the beast. 'I sheltered you, I fed you, and this is how you repay me!'

'Oh, good sir,' cried the unlucky merchant, 'I meant no harm! I only took the flower for my daughter, Beauty. I promised her a gift from my travels.'

'I shall release you, merchant,' growled the beast, 'but on one condition. One of your daughters must come and live with me here.'

'But, sir, my daughters are all I have!' wept the merchant.

'Silence!' roared the beast. 'Go home. Describe me, truthfully. Tell your daughters of our bargain — one of them must come here of her own free will.' He looked at the merchant. 'Do not try to escape me, or my revenge will be terrible.'

With a heavy heart the merchant saddled his horse. But before he set off, the beast gave him the rose he had picked. 'You promised this to your daughter,' he said quietly.

When the merchant reached home his daughters gathered round in excitement. One by one he gave them their gifts — a fine dress, jewels, perfumes. With tears in his eyes he handed Beauty her rose.

'What is the matter, father?' asked Beauty. 'Why do you cry?'

The merchant described the enchanted castle and the terrible beast, and the awful promise he had made.

'None of this would have happened but for me,' said Beauty. 'I should never have asked for a rose in winter.' She vowed she would do what the beast had commanded.

Beauty and her father set off for the castle. A meal had been laid before the fire once more. After they had eaten, they heard a low growl. Beauty held on to her father, as the beast walked into the room.

ALTHOUGH BEAUTY WAS AFRAID OF HIM,
SHE TRIED NOT TO LET HER FEAR SHOW.

The merchant had described the beast well. Although Beauty was afraid of him, she tried not to let her fear show.

'Good evening, merchant,' said the beast. 'I see you have brought one of your daughters with you. What is your name, child?'

'I am called Beauty,' she replied.

'Well, Beauty, did you come of your own free will?'

'Yes, I did.'

'And if I release your father, will you stay with me?'

'Yes, I will,' said Beauty bravely.

'Then tomorrow, merchant,' said the beast, 'you leave here, never to return. But you shall be rewarded for your courage.'

He pointed to a trunk full of gold coins.

'Take as much as you can carry,' he said. Then he growled goodnight and left.

That night, Beauty had a strange dream. A handsome prince spoke to her, saying, 'Do not be afraid. You are brave and good and you shall be rewarded.'

In the morning, Beauty and her father wept as they said goodbye, but at last the merchant set off, his horse laden with gold.

Then the beast spoke.

'You are brave, Beauty,' he said. 'I have something for you. Come with me.'

He took her to his library, and showed her a mirror.

'Whenever you wish to see your family,' he said, 'just look into this glass.'

Beauty looked. At first all she could see was her own anxious face. Then the picture slowly dissolved. Now she could see her home, and she felt much better.

Time passed, and Beauty grew used to the beast. One morning, she found a note from him on her breakfast table. He asked to join her for supper.

That evening, the hall was lit by a thousand twinkling candles. Beauty and the beast talked easily

and happily. Then, suddenly, the beast leaned across the table and said, 'Beauty, will you marry me?'

Surprised, Beauty said, 'No, Beast, I cannot,' and fled from the room. That night, she dreamed again of the prince. 'Courage,' he said.

More time passed. Each evening Beauty dined with the beast, and when he looked at her, she saw a softness in his eyes. She was growing very fond of him.

She had lived with the beast for a little over a year, when she looked in the mirror one day to see her father sitting by the fire, looking sad, and lost. Her sisters had married and he was all alone.

Beauty begged the beast to let her go home but he roared and stamped. He couldn't bear the thought of her leaving. But he couldn't bear to see her suffer, and agreed to let her go. Beauty took the mirror with her, so that, from time to time, she might look into it and see the beast.

Her father was overjoyed to see her. But Beauty stayed longer than she meant to, and one night the young man appeared again in her dreams. 'Look in the mirror, and keep your courage,' he said. She looked into the glass, and there was the beast.

He was hunched against the wall where once the roses had grown. Now their petals were strewn across the gardens like snow. He was heartbroken.

Beauty was filled with love for the poor beast and left straight away for the castle. Deep in the forest her horse heard howling wolves and shied in fear. Beauty was thrown onto the ground. Yellow eyes stared at her, and she cried for help.

The beast heard her cry. He rushed out and fought the wolves until they ran away. But he was wounded, and after he had carried Beauty safely into his ruined garden, he collapsed. Beauty cradled him in her arms.

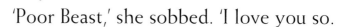
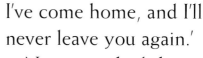

'Poor Beast,' she sobbed. 'I love you so. I've come home, and I'll never leave you again.'

No sooner had she spoken, than the air around them changed. The leaves turned green again, and a sparkling light glittered round the beast.

His features softened and changed. He became the handsome young man from her dream!

'Oh, Beauty! I have been under a wicked spell,' he cried. 'It could only be broken if someone told me she truly loved me. You have saved me. Please say you'll marry me?'

Beauty married her beast. They lived contentedly in the castle. And the merchant lived with them, and together they tended the white roses in the garden.

NOW THE DAY IS OVER

Now the day is over,
Night is drawing nigh,
Shadows of the evening
Steal across the sky.
Now the darkness gathers,
Stars begin to peep,
Birds and beasts and flowers
Soon will be asleep.

SABINE BARING GOULD

24

UP THE HILL TO BEDFORDSHIRE

Up the wooden hill
to Bedfordshire.

Down Sheet Lane
To Blanket Fair.

ANON.

25

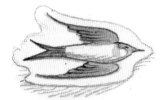

CALICO PIE

Calico Pie
The little Birds fly
Down to the calico tree.
Their wings were blue
And they sang 'Tilly-loo!'
Till away they flew —
And they never came back to me!
They never came back!
They never came back!
They never came back to me!

Calico Jam
The little Fish swam,
Over the syllabub sea.
He took off his hat,
To the Sole and the Sprat,
And the Willeby-Wat —
But he never came back to me!
He never came back!
He never came back!
He never came back to me!

Calico Ban
The little Mice ran,
To be ready in time for tea.
Flippity flup,
They drank it all up,
And danced in the cup —
But they never came back to me!
They never came back!
They never came back!
They never came back to me!

Calico Drum,
The Grasshoppers come,
The Butterfly, Beetle, and Bee
Over the ground,
Around and round,
With a hop and a bound —
But they never came back!
They never came back!
They never came back!
They never came back to me!

EDWARD LEAR

27

THE
FROG PRINCE

ONCE, LONG AGO, in a far off land of forests and
rivers, lived a good king. The king had many
daughters, and all had married fine princes. All except
Zinnia, his youngest and most beautiful daughter.
Zinnia, her father's favourite, grew up wilful and
difficult. The palace servants avoided her as
much as they could, in case she made
them do something unpleasant.

On hot summer days, Princess
Zinnia would walk under the
trees in the cool forest. One
morning, Zinnia took her
maid and made her watch
as she played catch with
a golden ball.

The ball looked so pretty,
catching the light as it flew.

It was an ancient and precious ball, and had been the king's favourite toy when he was little. Princess Zinnia had promised not to lose it, but she was growing reckless, throwing it further and higher, and every time it was lost from sight, the poor maid was sent to find it. The princess was playing near an old dark well, and pretty soon the maid guessed what would happen next. So she excused herself, and ran back towards the palace. She didn't want to have to crawl around in some dirty old well for the spoilt princess.

Princess Zinnia threw the ball up, and caught it. Threw it up, and caught it. Threw it up, and . . . missed!

The ball slipped through her fingers and

fell straight down the well. Zinnia looked round for her maid to fetch it, but she, of course, was well on her way back to the palace. Zinnia called out for help, but there was no one around. She reluctantly put her head into the dank mouth of the well.

Pulling aside the prickly weeds, she could just see the ball floating down at the bottom, lost. Her father would be furious.

Princess Zinnia felt so sorry for herself that she put her head in her hands and cried.

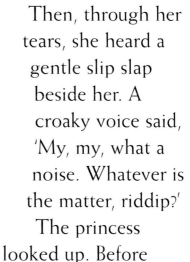

Wouldn't anybody help her?

Then, through her tears, she heard a gentle slip slap beside her. A croaky voice said, 'My, my, what a noise. Whatever is the matter, riddip?'

The princess looked up. Before her sat a big green frog.

She was so upset about the ball that she thought nothing of the fact that a frog had spoken to her.

'I've lost my gold ball at the bottom of the well. It is so deep and dirty and I could never fetch it back. My father, the king, will be so angry that I've lost it.'

SHE WAS SO UPSET ABOUT THE BALL THAT SHE THOUGHT
NOTHING OF THE FACT THAT A FROG HAD SPOKEN TO HER.

'You're a princess then?' asked the
frog. Zinnia nodded miserably. 'Don't
worry,' the frog said, 'I can get your
ball back for you.' And he hopped up
to the edge of the well.

'Of course,' he said, 'I shall want
something in return.'

'Anything at all,' said the princess. 'My
jewels, my crown, my silk dresses . . .'

'I don't have much use for jewels or silk
dresses,' said the frog. 'Instead you must
let me eat supper with you from your
golden plates, and drink some wine from
your own golden cup.'

'All right,' said Princess Zinnia.

'Also, I should like to sleep beside you
on your pillow,' said the frog.

'Yes, yes,' said the princess impatiently.
'Anything! Just fetch my ball back.'

'Very well,' said the frog, 'but a frog
needs a wife and a beautiful princess like
you would make me a fine wife. Will you
marry me as well? Then I will fetch the
ball back for you straight away, riddip.'

The princess was so shocked that she
stopped crying and stared at the frog
in horror. Marry a frog? *Marry a frog?*
The very idea!

Still, if she promised to marry it, then at least it would fetch the ball back.

'Oh, all right,' she said at last. 'I promise.'

The frog dived deep down into the dark. Soon he was back with the precious ball in his wide mouth. The princess snatched it and dashed off as fast as she could, without a word of thanks or another thought for the poor frog.

That evening, the king and Princess Zinnia were eating dinner, when they heard a tap on the door. A croaky voice said, 'Open up, lovely princess, and let me in, riddip.'

The princess left the table and peeped round the door. There was the frog. She slammed the door quickly.

'What on earth is it, my dear?' asked the king.

'Just a frog, father. It helped me today. In return I promised him he could eat with us.'

The king was secretly amused at this.

'Well,' he said, 'a promise is a promise. Let the frog in.'

So Zinnia had to open the door. The frog hopped up to the table. He shared the supper from their golden plates, and the wine from their golden cups.

At bedtime the frog hopped down and followed the
king and Princess Zinnia to the royal bedchambers.
The princess looked down in horror as the frog waited
outside her door.

'What is it now?' asked her father.

'I promised he could sleep on my pillow,' she said,
hoping her father would have the frog taken away.

But the king was enjoying this too much.

He answered as gravely as he could, 'Well, my dear,
a promise is a promise. Especially one given by a
princess to a frog.' So poor Zinnia had to let the frog
leap onto her pillow. When she was safely under the
covers, the frog spoke again.

'One last thing,' he said. 'I should so like you to kiss me, before we are married.'

Princess Zinnia was tempted to scream, but she knew her father would make her kiss the horrid thing anyway. Perhaps it would be better to get it over with.

She closed her eyes and leaned forward. She shivered as she touched the cold, damp creature. Then she suddenly felt a warmth and a softness she hadn't expected. She opened her eyes.

There stood a handsome young man!

Zinnia sat up in bed with a start, and pulled the covers up to her chin.

'Oh, thank heaven!' cried the young man. 'You have broken the spell put on me by a wicked sorceress. The spell could only be broken by a kiss from a beautiful princess.'

The king, hearing the commotion from outside, burst into the room. He was rather surprised to see the young man in place of the frog.

The princess explained how the young man had appeared, released from a spell by her kiss. He was, after all, a prince, so the king sent him off to sleep in a different part of the palace.

In good time, Princess Zinnia kept the promise she had made at the well, and married the Frog Prince.

And they were always kind to frogs — and even toads.

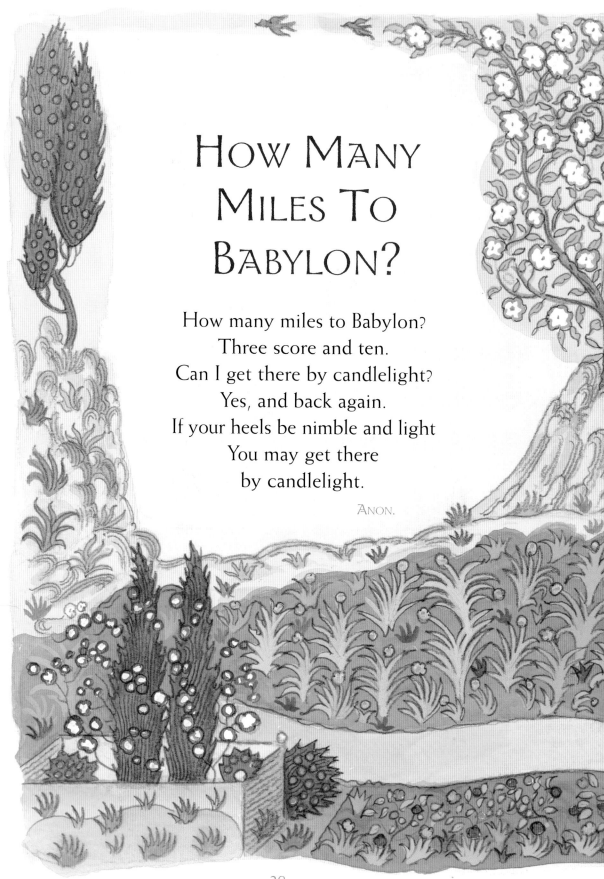

How Many Miles To Babylon?

How many miles to Babylon?
Three score and ten.
Can I get there by candlelight?
Yes, and back again.
If your heels be nimble and light
You may get there
by candlelight.

ANON.

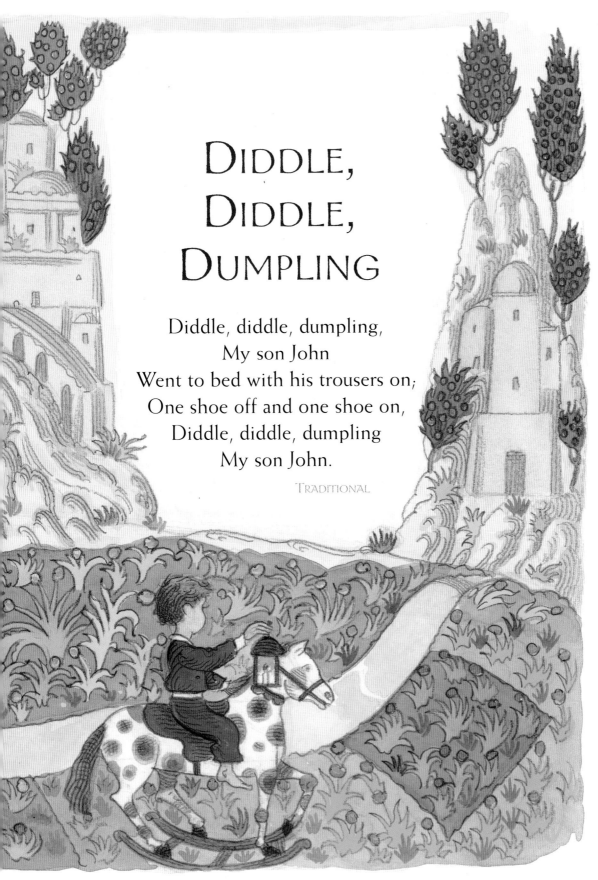

DIDDLE, DIDDLE, DUMPLING

Diddle, diddle, dumpling,
My son John
Went to bed with his trousers on;
One shoe off and one shoe on,
Diddle, diddle, dumpling
My son John.

TRADITIONAL

LULLABY

Hush a bye, baby
Daddy's away,
Brothers and sisters
Have gone out to play,
But here by your cradle,
Dear baby, I'll keep
To guard you from danger,
And sing you to sleep.

ANON.

40

TO THE MOON

Art thou pale for weariness
Of climbing heaven, and gazing on the earth,
Wandering companionless
Among the stars that have a different birth,
And ever-changing, like a joyless eye
That finds no object worth its constancy?

P. B. SHELLEY

THE LAND OF NOD

From breakfast on through all the day
At home among my friends I stay
But every night I go abroad
Afar into the Land of Nod.

All by myself I have to go,
With none to tell me what to do
All alone beside the streams
And up the mountainside of dreams.

The strangest things are there for me,
Both things to eat and things to see,
And many frightening sights abroad
Till morning in the Land of Nod.

Try as I like to find the way,
I can never get back by day,
Nor can remember plain and clear
The curious music that I hear.

ROBERT LOUIS STEVENSON

CINDERELLA

ONCE UPON A TIME, there lived a rich merchant, his wife and their daughter. They were very happy — until, after a sudden illness, the merchant's wife died. The merchant was afraid to be alone so he married again. His new wife had two daughters of her own.

The stepmother and her daughters were jealous of the merchant's daughter, and while he was away on business, they made the poor girl's life a misery. They kept the best of everything, while the merchant's daughter had to do all the cooking and cleaning.

Soon, she was so covered in dust and ashes from the fireplaces, they nicknamed her Cinderella. Poor Cinderella had to live in the kitchen, with only the mice for company.

One day, while the merchant was away, an invitation to a grand ball arrived from the palace. Cinderella's stepmother was beside herself with excitement. Here was a chance for her two girls to find themselves good husbands, and maybe even meet the prince.

Preparations began immediately. Dresses arrived every day for the sisters to approve. Each one was discarded.

'Pack this hideous dress away, will you?' they shouted at Cinderella. 'And tell the dressmaker she'll have to do better if she expects to be paid!'

Cinderella wistfully wrapped the dresses up, and sent them back. Once or twice she held an especially lovely dress against herself, and practised dancing in front of

the old mirror in the cellar. But this made her feel sad,
so she stopped.

Finally everything was ready. The dresses had at last
been chosen. The horses had been groomed and the
carriage was polished until it gleamed.

The sisters teased Cinderella. 'Such a shame about
your rags,' they said laughing cruelly, 'but then, ash
grey is quite the colour this season!'

Then they swept out leaving Cinderella all alone in
the kitchen.

Cinderella watched them from the window.

'How I wish I could have gone to the ball,' she
sighed. Then she sadly set about feeding the mice some
left-over cheese.

As she put the last lump down, a golden glow filled
the room. Brighter than moonlight, and warm as the
sun, it bathed the cold grey kitchen with shimmering
light. A finely dressed
lady appeared, shining
and radiant.

'Fear not, Cinderella,'
she said, smiling, 'for you
shall go to the ball. I am
your Fairy Godmother
and I will help you.'

Then she led
Cinderella out to the
vegetable patch.

'Fetch me that pumpkin,'
she said, and with a graceful
wave she turned it into a
shining golden coach.

'Now fetch me some
mice. About six should
do it.'

Cinderella returned
to the kitchen and
coaxed the mice out
from under the skirting
board. In the blink of an
eye four were turned into
white horses, while the
two remaining mice were
changed into a coachman
and a well-dressed footman.

'There,' said the Fairy
Godmother, 'everything is set.'

Cinderella was too dazzled to speak.
But she looked down sadly at her
tattered rags.

'Oh, silly me!' laughed the Fairy
Godmother. 'There!' And with that,
Cinderella's dirty clothes became a
beautiful silver dress.

Her hair was brushed and shining, and
she wore a perfume of jasmine and vanilla.

ON HER FEET WERE THE DAINTIEST OF GLASS SLIPPERS.

On her feet were the daintiest of glass slippers.

'Perfect,' said the lady. 'There's just one thing. Be sure to leave the ball before the clock strikes midnight. Now, go, and have a wonderful time!'

As she arrived at the ball, Cinderella covered her eyes with a mask, so her stepsisters wouldn't recognize her.

The prince, a kind boy known as Prince Charming, saw her at once. He bowed to her and asked if she would join him for the next dance. Cinderella agreed happily. She and the prince danced so beautifully, that her stepmother and stepsisters were driven to a fury of jealousy. 'Who is that girl?' they hissed. The prince danced for as long as he could with Cinderella, and as they danced, they talked. They liked all the same things. They seemed made for each other.

The prince was bewitched by the mysterious girl and they danced and danced in a dream of happiness.

All too soon, the clock began to strike.

One, two, three . . .

'I'm sorry, but I must go,' Cinderella gasped.

She ran away quickly. At the top of the stairs, she turned and looked round. The prince looked so puzzled — but she had no time to explain. She bolted down the outside steps, losing one of her pretty little slippers as she ran. But the clock was already striking ten. There was no time to pick it up.

She fell into her coach, and set off down the road. Behind her, the clock was striking. Eleven, twelve . . .

At the last stroke, the carriage dissolved around her and she fell onto the road. Her dress faded back to ashen rags and she found herself sitting amongst bits of broken pumpkin, with six white mice scurrying around her. Slowly, but happily, Cinderella made her way home.

The next morning, she waited on her stepmother and sisters cheerfully. She even put flowers on the table.

'Take them away,' groaned her stepmother.

She and Cinderella's stepsisters then spent the whole morning complaining about the mysterious girl from the ball.

'I'd like to give her a piece of my mind,' they said bitterly. 'Her with her airs and graces.'

Cinderella heard their complaints as she cleaned out the fireplaces, and hid her smiles.

Later that morning, there was a knock at the door. Cinderella was sent to open it. A footman from the palace was outside with a proclamation. He read its contents aloud in the drawing room.

'To all persons having attended the ball of the previous evening, draw near and hear this,' he said, grandly.

'Yes, yes, get on with it,' snapped Cinderella's stepmother. 'We haven't got all day.'

The footman drew himself up to his full height and continued, 'It is announced that Prince Charming seeks the girl he danced with at the aforementioned ball. The prince has in his possession a glass slipper left behind by the young lady in question. The prince will visit each household and all women of marriageable age are invited to try on the slipper. Whomsoever the slipper fits, the prince will marry.'

He folded the declaration carefully, and put it away.

Then, stopping only to glare at Cinderella's stepmother, he swept out of the house.

'Oh, Mama!' squeaked the stepsisters. 'How exciting! The slipper is sure to fit one of us — we have such pretty feet!'

'I'm sure it will be me,' said the eldest. 'Just look at my slim ankles.'

'No, no,' said her sister. 'It's bound to be me. My feet have such a fine shape.'

As they squabbled, their mother bundled Cinderella downstairs into the cellar.

'Don't you go getting any fancy ideas,' she said harshly. 'Don't even think about trying on that slipper. Stay here and scrub this floor until it shines!'

Then she slammed the door, and locked Cinderella in.

Cinderella broke down and cried. How could she show the prince that the slipper belonged to her?

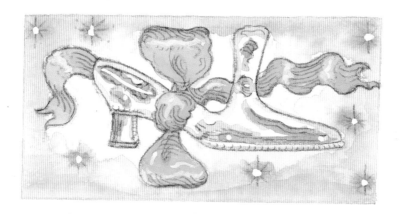

That evening, the prince drew up in his golden car. He was in despair. No one had come near to fitting the dainty slipper. His beautiful girl had simply vanished into thin air.

He was ushered into the drawing room, where the two stepsisters sat on the sofa in their stockinged feet. The prince hoped the slipper would not fit.

The eldest sister crammed her toes as hard as she could into the little shoe, but her big toe bulged out. She burst into tears.

Her sister grabbed the slipper. She tried as hard as she could to twist her foot into the shoe, but her heel burst over the edge. She too burst into tears.

The prince looked on sadly. 'Are there no other girls in this house?' he asked. The stepmother shook her head firmly.

The prince was just about to leave when a tall gentleman came into the drawing room. It was Cinderella's father, back at last from his business trip.

The prince bowed, explained why he was there, and then said, 'Sadly, I must now leave, as neither of these two young ladies fit the slipper, and there are no others in your household.'

'But what of my own daughter?' asked the merchant, puzzled. 'Where is she? Has she not tried the slipper?'

'Well, she was not at the ball, my dearest,' said his wife quickly.

'Why not?' he demanded, beginning to wonder what had been going on while he was away.

The prince cut in. 'All shall try the slipper,' he said. 'Bring the girl here at once.'

At this the stepsisters cried even harder, and their mother turned very red.

Cinderella was delighted to see her beloved father again. He was distressed to see her ragged dress, and her tattered stockings, but he brought her into the drawing room all the same.

The prince looked carefully at the smudged and grimy face before him. He thought he could see something familiar, something that made his heart flutter.

THE PRINCE HIMSELF PLACED THE LITTLE GLASS SLIPPER
ON TO HER FOOT. IT FITTED PERFECTLY.

Cinderella smiled at him. The prince himself placed
the little glass slipper on to her foot. It fitted perfectly.

The stepsisters fell to the floor, screaming. Their
mother left the drawing room, and went off to pack.
She did not think she would be staying much longer
in that house. Cinderella's father blinked in surprise.

And Cinderella? She fell into the prince's arms,
and together they waltzed around the room in a daze
of delight.

'Issue a new proclamation!' laughed the prince to the
startled footman. 'Announce a royal wedding!'

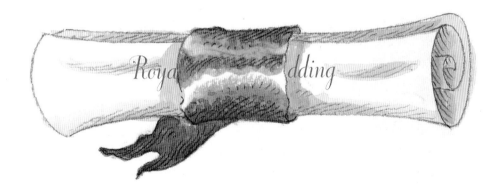

Cinderella married her prince, and for the rest of
their lives they lived and danced together in happiness.

WYNKEN, BLYNKEN, AND NOD

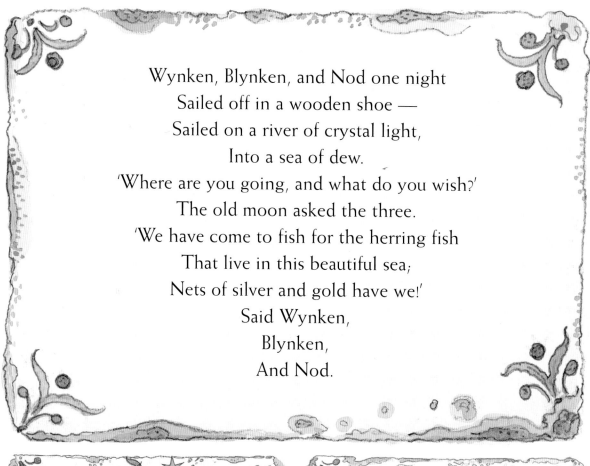

Wynken, Blynken, and Nod one night
Sailed off in a wooden shoe —
Sailed on a river of crystal light,
Into a sea of dew.
'Where are you going, and what do you wish?'
The old moon asked the three.
'We have come to fish for the herring fish
That live in this beautiful sea;
Nets of silver and gold have we!'
Said Wynken,
Blynken,
And Nod.

The old moon laughed and sang a song,
As they rocked in the wooden shoe,
And the wind that sped them all night long
Ruffled the waves of dew.
The little stars were the herring fish
That lived in that beautiful sea —
'Now cast your nets where you wish —'
So cried the stars to the fishermen three:
Wynken,
Blynken,
And Nod.

All night long their nets they threw
To the stars in the twinkling foam —
Then down from the skies came the wooden shoe,
Bringing the fishermen home;
'Twas all so pretty a sail it seemed
As if it could not be,
And some folk thought 'twas a dream they'd dreamed
Of sailing that beautiful sea —
But I shall name you the fishermen three:
Wynken,
Blynken,
And Nod.

Wynken and Blynken are two little eyes,
And Nod is a little head,
And the wooden shoe that sailed the skies
Is the wee one's trundle bed.
So shut your eyes while mother sings
Of wonderful sights that be,
And you shall see the beautiful things
As you rock in the misty sea,
Where the old shoe rocked the fishermen three:
Wynken,
Blynken,
And Nod.

EUGENE FIELD

THE EMPEROR AND THE NIGHTINGALE

ONCE, IN FAR OFF CHINA, there lived a wealthy emperor. His gardens were famous throughout the world for their beauty, and kings and queens came to marvel at their silver fountains and exotic flowers.

Just beyond the gardens lay a dark forest. In the forest there lived a nightingale. Her song was clear and tender, and whoever heard it immediately stopped what they were doing to listen.

One day the emperor was proudly showing off some new fountains when his visitors suddenly stopped.

'Can you hear the song of that nightingale?' said one.

The emperor, annoyed, replied, 'Yes, but surely it cannot compare to these fountains?'

'Oh, they are indeed magnificent,' his other visitor agreed, 'but just listen to that song. It is enough to break your heart.'

That evening the emperor summoned his chamberlain.

'Bring the nightingale here at once,' he commanded.

The chamberlain had no idea how to trap a nightingale. In despair, he went to the royal chef. Perhaps he would know how to catch them for food. The chef could not be found, but the kitchen maid said she knew the nightingale very well.

'I listen to her every night on my way home,' she said.

The little kitchen maid led the chamberlain into the forest and they waited. Soon they heard the pure, sweet song of the nightingale.

'There she is,' said the kitchen maid, and she pointed to the little grey bird.

'That drab little thing?' spluttered the chamberlain.

Undeterred, the kitchen maid called up to the bird, 'Little nightingale, our great emperor longs to hear you sing. Will you come with us to the palace?'

'It would be an honour,' the nightingale replied.

The emperor sat on his grandest porcelain throne. Everything had been carefully arranged for the nightingale's song — a special golden perch had been set up next to the throne, and the whole court waited for the performance to start. The emperor pointed loftily to indicate that it was time for the little bird to begin.

The nightingale opened her throat and poured out her song, liquid silver and pure. Tears of happiness filled the emperor's eyes.

'You shall be rewarded with gold and jewels!' he cried. 'The finest my empire can provide.'

'I have had my reward,' the bird replied. 'An emperor has shed tears at my song, and that is enough for me.'

The emperor could not be dissuaded, however, and the nightingale was quickly appointed an official of the court. All day she sat on her golden perch to sing.

One morning a messenger arrived at the palace bearing a gift from the emperor of Japan, wrapped in rose-coloured tissue paper.

The emperor tore off the wrapping, and opened the box. Inside he found a toy nightingale, made of bright silk feathers encrusted with jewels.

'A gift from the emperor of Japan,' read the attached note. 'A poor nightingale compared to the nightingale of the emperor of China.'

ONE MORNING A MESSENGER ARRIVED AT THE PALACE BEARING A GIFT
FROM THE EMPEROR OF JAPAN, WRAPPED IN ROSE-COLOURED TISSUE PAPER.

The chamberlain wound up the toy. It sang the same song as the real nightingale, but with such precision and regularity that the emperor could sing along. He was delighted, and clapped his hands.

'This beautiful bird must sing a duet with our own grey friend,' he declared, but the nightingale had flown away.

The mechanical bird sang every evening. People gathered in the palace courtyard at sunset to listen to the little toy's song, and were amazed by its beauty. There were only a few who muttered that something wasn't quite right.

The emperor was enchanted with his toy, and gave it a special seat of golden cushions.

One evening, he was enjoying the song when the little bird suddenly started to wrench and click. Then there was no song. The music had stopped.

After much trouble, the court clockmaker mended the bright little toy. He warned the emperor that it should be used only rarely, for it was now weak and would break for ever if used too often. The emperor was only able to listen to the precious songs of the toy nightingale on one day a year.

Five years passed, and, without the sound of the nightingale's song, the emperor grew weary and heartsick. He retired to his bed. Day after day he lay, barely moving, growing paler and weaker as each day passed. The little toy bird stood silently on its cushion.

A dark figure sat wrapped in a black cloak next to the great bed. It was Death, waiting patiently beside the emperor, in case he was needed. When the emperor saw him, he cried out in great fear, 'Oh, precious bird, music, please, some music, some life, I beg you! After all I have given you, little bird, please, just one of your songs!'

But there was no music, and there was no one there to wind the key.

Suddenly, there came the sound of tinkling silver song. The drab forest nightingale had heard about the dying emperor and had flown back to sing for him again.

She sang for a long time, and her sweet melody floated through the window. As she sang, the dark figure beside the bed faded and vanished.

The emperor sat up for the first time in weeks and called out in joy, 'Oh, little nightingale, why did I banish you? Your song has brought me back to life. How can I ever reward you?'

'I have already had my reward, as I have told you before,' said the nightingale. 'Your tears are reward enough for me,' and she sang once more, as the emperor fell into a deep and peaceful sleep.

When he awoke, he saw the nightingale perched on the window ledge.

'Please stay here with me,' he begged. 'I shall have that wretched toy bird smashed into pieces.'

'It did its best,' said the nightingale. 'Do not punish it. I cannot live in your palace again, for I belong out in the wild forest, but I shall come often and sing for you, just as I sing for the little kitchen maid.'

And with that the little nightingale flew away. Then the emperor rose and dressed himself for the first time in a year. He felt alive again — more than alive.

At last, he felt happy.

THE TYGER

Tyger! Tyger! burning bright
In the forests of the night,
What immortal hand or eye
Could frame thy fearful symmetry?

WILLIAM BLAKE

THE MOUSE'S LULLABY

Oh rock-a-by, baby Mouse, rock-a-by, so!
When baby's asleep to the baker's I'll go,
And while he's not looking I'll pop from a hole,
And bring to my baby a fresh penny roll.

PALMER COX

BABY BEDS

Little lambs, little lambs
Where do you sleep?
'In the green meadow
With mother sheep.'
Little birds, little birds
Where do you rest?
'Close to our mother
In a warm nest.'
Baby dear, baby dear,
Where do you lie?
'In my warm bed
With mother close by.'

ANON.

SLEEPING BEAUTY

ONCE UPON A TIME, in an age of magic, there lived a king and queen. All was well with their lives, except for one thing. They longed for a child.

One day, the queen was out walking in the royal forest, when she saw an ermine caught in a trap. She knelt and released the delicate creature.

Instead of dashing away, the little ermine whispered to the queen.

'Because of your kindness,' it said, 'your greatest wish shall be granted.'

And with that, like quicksilver, it disappeared.

Sure enough, the king and queen were soon blessed with a beautiful baby daughter. Brimming over with happiness, they planned a party for the little girl's naming day.

Invitations were sent out to everyone in the kingdom, including wizards and fairies. There were twelve good fairies living in the kingdom at that time, but also one bad fairy. She lived in the shadows and was the only one not to be invited.

During the naming ceremony for the baby Princess Aurora all the good fairies bestowed virtues and qualities like wisdom, grace, and beauty onto the child. One after the other they blessed her.

The twelfth fairy, Bluebell, was just about to offer her gift, when the door to the castle crashed open. The bad fairy Bindweed slid into the room like a plume of dark smoke.

She floated over to where Aurora lay sleeping. 'I see you are all enjoying yourselves,' she hissed.

'My invitation must have got lost.'

The king opened his mouth to speak, but with a wave of her arm Bindweed silenced him.

'You have all given of your best to this sweet, innocent baby,' she cackled, 'and I shall do the same. When the princess reaches her sixteenth birthday, she will pierce her finger on a spindle . . . and she will die!'

The king and queen stared in horror as Bindweed slithered out of the door.

A silence fell over the party.

'Excuse me, your majesties,' said Bluebell at last, 'but I have not yet given little Aurora my gift. I cannot undo the dreadful spell cast on her, but I can temper it a little. The princess will not die if she pricks her finger, but instead will sleep for a hundred years, or until she is awakened by the kiss of true love.'

That same day, the king gave orders for all spinning wheels to be burnt, and passed a law banishing spindles and needles for ever.

The princess grew up happy, graceful, and kind.

The time soon came for her sixteenth birthday party. Great preparations were made. Candle lanterns were hung in the trees. The palace kitchens created a magnificent birthday feast. Everyone was so busy that they didn't notice that Princess Aurora was missing.

She had been practising her dancing in a remote corridor, when she passed a twisty staircase she had never seen before. It led to a dark tower.

At the top of the stairs was a door with a tiny key in the lock. A strange sound was coming from behind it. Aurora turned the key, and opened the door.

She saw a little old lady sitting behind a spinning wheel. Aurora had never seen a spinning wheel before and was curious.

'May I have a look?' she asked politely.

'Of course,' said the old lady, smiling.

She handed Aurora the machine's silver spindle. As Aurora took it, the point pierced her finger. A bright bead of blood welled up, and the princess immediately fell onto a bed in a corner of the room, asleep.

The old lady, cackling horribly, twisted herself into a plume of black smoke, and vanished.

All over the palace everyone, and everything, fell instantly asleep. The king, who had been practising his archery, curled up snoring on the royal lawn.

The royal guards slumped against the walls. The palace was completely under Bindweed's wicked enchantment.

Year after year they slept. Rose bushes thick with bright flowers and sharp thorns grew over the walls. Soon the whole palace was hidden — all except for the top of the tower, which peeped out over the briars.

The legend of the sleeping princess grew, and many tried to get into the palace. But the roses were too thick and prickly to cut through.

Years passed, and Princess Aurora and her sleeping palace were almost forgotten. Only the older people sometimes remembered and told travellers the strange tale.

One night, a prince from a far country stopped at a

nearby inn where he was told the story. He liked a challenge, so he set off early next morning, and soon found the wall of tangled thorns and roses. He hacked his way through the thicket all that day, then the next, and the next.

On the third day, which was Aurora's birthday, he suddenly saw the tower pointing up through the briars. He redoubled his efforts and made his way to the palace gates. He passed the snoring guards, and tiptoed past the king who remained fast asleep on the lawn.

The prince fought his way to the tower, where he found the sleeping princess. The silver spindle lay by her side.

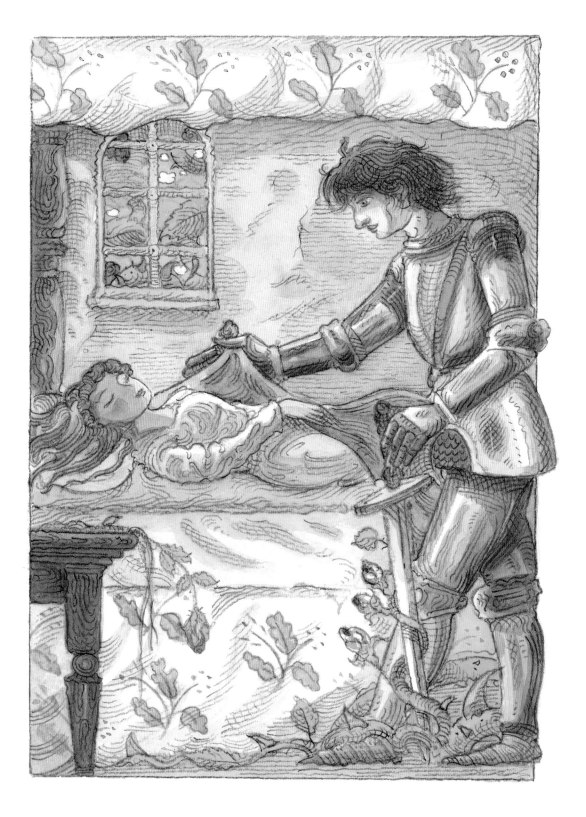

THE PRINCE FOUGHT HIS WAY TO THE TOWER,
WHERE HE FOUND THE SLEEPING PRINCESS.

A pale rose pink flushed her cheek. For the prince, it was love at first sight. He leaned forward, and kissed her gently. Aurora stirred, and her eyes fluttered open.

'I must have slept for ages,' she yawned. 'I dreamed so many wonderful dreams.' Then she looked at the prince. 'I'm sure I saw you in some of them,' she said, smiling.

At once, the whole palace came back to life as if it had never been asleep. The prince brought Princess Aurora down from her high turret, and the happy pair announced their intention to marry.

The palace bells were rung. And Aurora's birthday party became, instead, the joyous celebration of a royal wedding.

SLEEP BABY SLEEP

Sleep baby sleep,
Your father tends the sheep,
Your mother shakes the dreamland tree
And softly fall sweet dreams for thee,
Sleep baby sleep.

ANON.

EVENING

Hush hush little baby
The sun's in the west
The lamb in the meadow
Has lain down to rest.

The bough rocks the bird now
The flower rocks the bee,
The wave rocks the lily,
The wind rocks the tree.

And I rock the baby
So softly to sleep.
She must not awaken
Till daisy-buds peep.

ANON.

FROM A MIDSUMMER NIGHT'S DREAM

Philomel with melody,
Sing in our sweet lullaby;
Lulla, lulla, lullaby; lulla, lulla, lullaby.
Never harm
Nor spell nor charm
Come our lovely lady nigh.
So goodnight, with lullaby.

WILLIAM SHAKESPEARE

SEAL LULLABY

Oh! Hush thee, my baby,
The night is behind us,
And black are the waters
That sparkled so green.
The moon, o'er the combers,
Looks downward to find us
At rest in the hollows
That rustle between.

Where billow meets billow,
Then soft be thy pillow,
Ah, weary wee flipperling, curl at thy ease.
The storm shall not wake thee,
Nor shark overtake thee,
Asleep in the arms
Of the slow-swinging seas.

RUDYARD KIPLING

INDEX

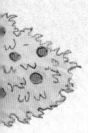